ATOS Book Level: __1.6__
AR Points: __0.5__
Quiz #: __164012__ ☑RP ☐ LS ☐ VP
Lexile: _____

Dear Parent:

Congratulations! Your child is taking the first steps on an exciting journey. The destination? Independent reading!

STEP INTO READING® will help your child get there. The program offers five steps to reading success. Each step includes fun stories and colorful art. There are also Step into Reading Sticker Books, Step into Reading Math Readers, Step into Reading Phonics Readers, Step into Reading Write-In Readers, and Step into Reading Phonics Boxed Sets—a complete literacy program with something to interest every child.

Learning to Read, Step by Step!

Ready to Read   Preschool–Kindergarten
• big type and easy words • rhyme and rhythm • picture clues
For children who know the alphabet and are eager to begin reading.

Reading with Help   Preschool–Grade 1
• basic vocabulary • short sentences • simple stories
For children who recognize familiar words and sound out new words with help.

Reading on Your Own   Grades 1–3
• engaging characters • easy-to-follow plots • popular topics
For children who are ready to read on their own.

Reading Paragraphs   Grades 2–3
• challenging vocabulary • short paragraphs • exciting stories
For newly independent readers who read simple sentences with confidence.

Ready for Chapters   Grades 2–4
• chapters • longer paragraphs • full-color art
For children who want to take the plunge into chapter books but still like colorful pictures.

STEP INTO READING® is designed to give every child a successful reading experience. The grade levels are only guides. Children can progress through the steps at their own speed, developing confidence in their reading, no matter what their grade.

Remember, a lifetime love of reading starts with a single step!

To all my high-flying friends!
—F.B.

Step into Reading, Random House, and the Random House colophon are registered trademarks of Random House, Inc.

Visit us on the Web!
StepIntoReading.com
randomhouse.com/kids

Educators and librarians, for a variety of teaching tools, visit us at RHTeachersLibrarians.com

ISBN 978-0-7364-3050-0 (trade) — ISBN 978-0-7364-8136-6 (lib. bdg.)

Printed in the United States of America 10 9 8 7 6 5 4 3 2 1

STEP INTO READING®

STEP 1

Disney

PLANES

PLANE PALS

By Frank Berrios

Illustrated by the Disney Storybook Artists

Random House 🏠 New York

Dusty is a crop duster.

Dusty wants

to be a racer!

His best friend,
Chug, helps him.

Dottie fixes planes.
If Dusty breaks down,
Dottie can fix him!

Skipper is a flying ace.

Ripslinger is
a racing champ.

Dusty will be
in a big race.
His friends cheer!

The race begins!
Dusty meets
other racing planes.

They have come from
all over the world.

El Chupacabra is
from Mexico.
He wears a mask
and a cape!

Bulldog is from England.

Franz is a car
from Germany.

He can turn into a plane!

Dusty learns
about racing
from his new friends.

Dusty gets racing tips
from Ishani.

She is a racing plane
from India.

Before long,

Dusty is in first place!

Fans all over the world
cheer for Dusty!

Ripslinger is jealous of Dusty.

Zed helps Ripslinger
cheat.

He bumps Dusty.

Dusty meets fighter jets
named Echo and Bravo.
They help him.

After a storm,

Dusty cannot fly.

Ishani wants to help.

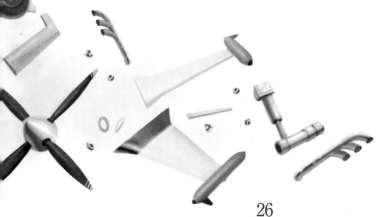

All his new friends help!

Dusty flies so fast!
Ned and Zed try
to make Dusty crash.

Skipper comes
to the rescue!

Dusty flies high
above Ripslinger.

Dusty wins!

Thanks to
his plane pals,
Dusty is a racer at last!